Everyone is Good
for Something

By Beatrice Schenk de Regniers

Pictures by Margot Tomes

 Houghton Mifflin/Clarion Books/New York

for D X F with love

Houghton Mifflin/Clarion Books,
52 Vanderbilt Ave., New York, NY 10017
Text copyright © 1979, 1980 by Beatrice Schenk de Regniers
Pictures copyright © 1980 by Margot Tomes

Library of Congress Cataloging in Publication Data

de Regniers, Beatrice Schenk.
  Everyone is good for something.

  "A Clarion book."
  Summary: Everyone tells the Boy he's good for nothing
until he rescues a wise cat and helps save an island
from a plague of mice.
  I. Tomes, Margot. II. Title.
PZ7.D4417Ev   [Fic]   79-12223   ISBN 0-395-28967-X

There was this boy. His mother said he was
good for nothing. And so the boy, too, thought
he was good for nothing.

And he really didn't seem to be good for much.

The boy's father was dead, and his mother was poor,
and the boy and his mother often went hungry.
This happened long ago,
in the days when you never knew what good thing or
what bad thing might happen next.

Try to get a job,
dear. We need
the money.

One cold winter day there was only a bit of bread
in the house. The boy's mother gave him his
father's warm sheepskin coat and sent him to town
to look for work.

The boy asked one person and then another for work.
But nobody wanted to hire him. At last the boy
decided he might as well go home.

On the way, he saw a scarecrow. It was dressed in rags that blew every which way in the cold wind.

"Oh, you poor thing!" the boy said. And he took off his sheepskin coat and put it on the scarecrow.

So the boy came home without a job and without his coat, and you can imagine the kind of welcome he got.

Try to get a job.

When summer came, the boy's mother gave him his
father's straw hat to keep the sun off his head
and sent him to town to look for work.

Nobody wanted to hire him, and the boy decided
he might as well go home.

Oh, you poor thing!

What will Mama say?

On the way, he saw a donkey standing in the hot sun. The boy felt so sorry for the donkey, he took off his father's straw hat and put it on the donkey's head.

Now the boy was in no hurry to go home without a job —and without a hat, too. So he sat down under a tree to rest.

Along came a man holding a sack in one hand and a penny in the other.

The man said he had a good-for-nothing cat in the sack. He told the boy to drown the cat and keep the penny. The boy took the penny, and he took the sack, and he set out for the river.

Oh, you poor thing!

FRESH FISH

Meow

When the boy got to the river, he untied the sack to take a look at the cat.

Well of course he was not going to throw her into the river—the poor thing! She looked so hungry, he took the penny and bought her some fish.

The boy wanted to take the cat home with him. But he didn't think his mother would like that. So the boy and the cat walked along the riverbank.

They came to a little sailboat. The cat jumped
on board and waited for the boy to come, too.

Now the boy knew he must go home sooner or later.
He thought a little later might be better.
So he followed the cat onto the boat.

The wind began to blow, and the boat began to
move out to sea. The boy felt so sleepy
he could not keep his eyes open.

Good morning,
Cat.

Good morning,
Jack.

See that island?
You will make
your fortune there.

When the boy woke up, he didn't know if it was a
day later or a year later. The cat was steering
the boat, heading for an island nearby.

The boy said good morning to the cat, and he wasn't
a bit surprised when she said, "Good morning, Jack."

But I'm good for nothing. I can't do anything.

Yes you can, Jack. You saved my life. I will help you.

But you are a good-for-nothing cat. The man said so.

Everyone is good for something!

The cat told Jack he would make his fortune on the island.
She promised to help him because he had saved her life.

The cat sailed the boat into the harbor, and
Jack stepped ashore. He soon learned that
there was trouble on the island.

We have too many mice.

We can't make our fine cheese anymore.

We used to be famous for our cheese.

It was overrun with mice, and people could not work or sleep or eat in peace. They asked Jack to help them.

Jack wanted to help. A cat would be good for chasing mice, he told them. But no one on the island had ever heard of cats.

Jack went back to the boat and asked the cat if she was willing to rid the island of mice. She was.

So they went ashore together, and the cat chased
all the mice into the sea.

The people wanted to keep the cat. As the cat
was willing, Jack agreed to leave her there.
He took a boatload of cheese in exchange.

Jack said good-by to the cat, and the cat
whispered something in his ear.

Now the wind began to blow, and the boat
began to move out to sea. Jack felt so sleepy,
he could not keep his eyes open.

When Jack woke up, he didn't know if it was a
day later or a year later. But there he was,
back on the river, not far from home.

Jack remembered the cat, and he remembered what
she had told him. Then he unloaded the boat
and sold the cheese.

Jack!

Mama!

Where have you been
all this time?

Now Jack went home with one bag full of cheese and
two bags full of money. His mother was glad to see him
after all that time. She was glad to see the money, too.

Jack bought a fine big farm for himself and his mother.

In winter, the scarecrows on his farm wore sheepskin coats.

In summer, the donkeys on his farm wore straw hats.

No one who came to Jack's door went away hungry.

And Jack and his mother lived in plenty—and in peace, most of the time.

A note from the author

There are heroes who set out to win fame and fortune. But I tend to be drawn to those who seem to drift from misfortune to fortune, and who achieve success—if achieve is not too strong a word—simply because they are open to whatever may happen; not a fashionable philosophy in our time, but one that has long endured.

Tales of men, women, or children who make their fortune when they provide a cat to people on a remote island plagued by mice were current long before the legend of Dick Whittington and his cat, and in many countries other than England. The motif is found in Danish popular tradition, in a thirteenth-century Italian chronicle, and as a Persian legend. Stith Thompson says it existed as a literary tale as early as the twelfth century.

The story as told here had its origin in a Russian tale I read long ago (and have never been able to find since) in which the feckless hero goes from adventure to adventure. Only this first adventure of the Russian version stayed with me—and somehow reshaped itself to the dimensions of my own fears, wishes, memories.

Every folktale retold becomes a kind of autobiography. I am, in part, the boy, the mother, the cat. And so is the reader. So are we all. That accounts, I think, for the universal appeal of these stories.